ALL PROFITS TO

YOUNG PEOPLE'S MENTAL HEALTH

CHARITIES

A special thank you to the staff at
Healthwatch Milton Keynes all the volunteers who give
their time to people with mental health issues. A really
special thank you to David Vaughan for his wonderful
illustrations, his professional help and guidance.

Lastly my wife Angela for all the help with this book. Plus
giving me the strength to keep carrying on.

Published by John Southall
Printed in Great Britain

ISBN 978 1 527263 54 3

TIMOTHY THE TORTOISE

AND

NANNY JANE HAS AN ADVENTURE

Timothy the Tortoise

Milton Keynes in Buckinghamshire England was changing from a sleepy town into a very busy city.

Mummies and Daddies were working so hard that they had little time to spare in their busy lives

Unbeknown to our world a Satellite was circling earth. The Satellite noticed that the mummies and daddies of Milton Keynes were getting very frustrated because of their busy lives.

The Satellite decided to send down to earth their robotic delivery vehicle, Timothy the Tortoise. The delivery vehicle would help the mummies and daddies with shopping of fresh fruit, fresh vegetables and special treats.

On their arrival in Milton Keynes the mummies and daddies made great use of the delivery vehicles. So much so that the mummies and daddies had much more time to play with their children. The children loved and adored Timothy. He had lights on his face, an orange pendant at the top of his head and tail, that glowed and he spoke as well.

The children loved Timothy so much that when they saw him, they would run and gather round him so excitedly. You would hear their shrieks of laughter and excitement such a long way off.

In Oakgrove, Milton Keynes, the Gray family were having breakfast but mummy started feeling a bit different. Daddy said we have to get grandma round because daddy has to take mummy to hospital.

When the children came home from school daddy told them that they had a new little sister. They were so excited they couldn't get to sleep. They were so tired that when daddy came to wake them up in the morning it took ages. It also took them so long to get washed and dressed and clean their teeth.

With all the excitement of the arrival of his new baby daughter, daddy had forgotten about breakfast for his other children. Daddy didn't know what to do. He told the children that there was no breakfast and how sorry he was.

The children rushed to their daddy shouting "don't worry, don't worry Timothy will bring it for us. He brings porridge, cereals, fruit and yoghurt."

Daddy was a little confused, "Who is Timothy?"

"He's the robotic Tortoise who brings things for all the busy mummies and daddies. You only have to use your phone and he will deliver."

Daddy did this and half an hour later daddy's phone rang to say Timothy was on his way.

Daddy and the children gathered outside their house and Timothy came rolling up the street. Timothy stopped right outside their house, but daddy had a problem opening Timothy's lid.

Timothy quickly realised that there was a problem and told daddy to phone the satellite. Daddy did this and the satellite managed to open Timothy's lid. Daddy had to speak to the satellite himself because they had the special code that would open Timothy's lid.

The children took their breakfast of cereal, fruit and yoghurt. Daddy took his porridge and bottle of skimmed milk. He then closed Timothy's lid and sent him on his way, but not before the children could give Timothy lots of hugs and kisses. Timothy had made their day a whole lot better. He had saved their day.

Timothy said good bye and went on his way ready to make another family happy. The satellite congratulated Timothy.

Timothy's next assignment was to a very old lady. She was known as Nanny Jane. Nanny Jane lived in a bungalow in Middleton village. Nanny Jane was very old and frail.

Timothy was able to enter Nanny Jane's bungalow because she had a special lock that was activated by laser beam from Timothy.

Nanny Jane loved her visits from Timothy especially when he arrived with special treats that her family had ordered.

Her family had decided that because they couldn't see her every day, they would employ the services of Timothy.

Timothy was able to visit Nanny Jane every day, he could spend time with her reading her books she liked. He could read her the newspaper. They could listen to music.

She would offer Timothy some of her treats forgetting that Timothy was a robot. To her he was a really good friend. So, she would give Timothy a pat and say thank you for coming to see me. An hour had past and Nanny Jane was feeling very tired.

She looked at Timothy and said "I think you best be off now Timothy; I am feeling very tired. Thank you for coming and making me very happy. I will see you next time."

Timothy looked up at Nanny Jane and said goodbye. Timothy made his way out making sure to activate the lock as he left.

The satellite said well done to Timothy and to go back to base and await his next job.

Nanny Jane goes on an adventure

Nanny Jane sat in her bungalow in Middleton Village and she was feeling very lonely. Timothy was not due to come on one of his visits today. She was starting to feel so alone and sad. Timothy did make her so happy when he came around on his visits. Near to tears she said to herself "come on Jane cheer up you'll see Timothy tomorrow." With that she fell to sleep in her armchair.

Suddenly she was awoken with the sound of children's laughter. "Nanny Jane, Nanny Jane, hello, hello." It was Nathan and Jane with their mummy. School had been closed for the day and mummy had to be at a meeting. It was a very important meeting for her work. Mummy just could not take the day off to look after Nathan and Jane. Mummy took the children round to Nanny Jane's to ask her if the children could keep her company. Nathan and Jane were twins and of an age not to be a trouble to Nanny Jane.

Nanny Jane said she would be delighted to have the children for company. Nobody knew how Nanny Jane was feeling and that this was the best thing that could have had happened to her today. Nathan Jane and Nanny Jane said goodbye to mummy.

"Well what would you two scallywags like to do today?" "No Nanny, what would you like to do?" "Well children there is something I would like to do, but I am never going to be able to do it." "What is that?" "I have heard that there are a great many things you can do at Willen Lake. I would love to have gone there but I am not going to be able to do it." "Why not?"said Nathan "Yes why not?" echoed Jane. "Because nobody has the time to take me," said Nanny Jane

Nathan and Jane felt very sad on hearing Nanny Jane say this. After a little time thinking Jane lifted her head and said "Nanny, Nanny, I know who can take you." "Who?" said Nanny Jane, "Why Timothy of course." "But he is a robot and can only do limited things." "That's what you think Nanny."

"How will we get Timothy here today he is not due to visit?" "Don't worry Nanny we have a special number. Can we use your mobile to contact Timothy?" "Yes off course" The children phoned the number and ordered Timothy's assistance.

Timothy came straight away smoothly negotiating the roads. On arrival at Nanny Jane's Bungalow he used his laser key to enter the property. Timothy was surprised to see the children were there. "Timothy we are so glad you came, Nanny is feeling very sad today and we need you to help." "Ok I will read the newspaper." "No" said the children together. "We want you to use your special powers. We want you to help us take Nanny Jane on an adventure. We want you to take her on your back over to Willen Lake." "Oh, that's simple but how did you know about my special powers," "let's just say we believe in you."

Timothy started transforming himself. His body started rising, two footplates came out of his sides, a harness came from his tail end and would wrap around his neck.

"Come on Nanny Jane get a coat on and off we go."
Nathan and Jane helped Nanny Jane out of her
armchair and put her coat on for her. They gave Nanny
Jane her walking stick and Timothy trundled up to
the side of her with the help of the children. Timothy
managed to securely seat Nanny Jane.

They were off, the children running alongside Timothy.
It was ok for the children to be out because they were
actually out with Nanny.

Nanny Jane was so happy it had been such a long time since she felt fresh air on her face. They meandered through the woods alongside the stream then over the bridge. Then Timothy came to an abrupt stop. "What is the matter Timothy?" the children shouted "Railway lines, railway lines" was the reply. "It's ok Timothy the trains only run on weekends." "It doesn't matter safety first. When it is safe to go I will go." After a few minutes Timothy decided it was safe to go. They soon came upon the adventure playground where you can negotiate all kinds of walk ways at all different levels using ropes for your route. Nanny Jane really loved watching all the children excitedly enjoying their play.

Then they looked at all the boats and canoes on the lake. A member of staff came up to them and asked if Timothy would like to take Nanny Jane onto the lake using the new Raft. They all shouted in unison "YES!" Nanny Jane could not stop smiling. The raft glided slowly around the lake, going in between all the other boats and canoes. The Swans, Ducks and Geese came quacking up to the raft. They were so close up Nanny Jane felt she could actually touch them but being old and wise knew she shouldn't.

When that trip was over they continued their journey around the lake. The scouts were out selling their duck food and Nanny Jane said lets buy some and feed the ducks. "I am glad they have told people to stop feeding them bread; it is so bad for them." Nanny Jane noticed that the pick and mix stall was closed and said to Jane and Nathan sorry but it's only the birds who are being fed today the sweetie shop is closed.

Time was flying by and Nanny Jane said to the children "have five minutes on the swings and then we must get back." This they did and Nanny Jane said next time they would do the rest and even one day go to Gulliver's land. They quickly trundled home.

When they got home the children and Timothy helped Nanny Jane back into her armchair. Timothy then got back into his normal position and said goodbye to them all. Nanny Jane swears that as Timothy left he winked at her.

Mummy wasn't far behind. When she got in, she asked nanny if the children had been good and Nanny Jane replied "haven't heard a squeak out of them it's been so quiet here." Of course that was true because they hadn't been there all day. It was their secret to keep to themselves.

When they left, Nanny Jane sighed she certainly had an adventure. This day would keep her so happy for months to come. It had been such a joyous day she fell asleep in her chair and didn't wake up until breakfast.

Timothy was inspired by the delivery robots we see on our streets of Milton Keynes.

and Nanny Jane had an adventure